W9-ASQ-789

MADANI'S BEST GAME

Dedicated to Madani, Aziz,
Daouda, Solo, Khalid, Hamadi, Abdelhadi,
and all those young people who shared matches
and their lives with me.
And to Juan, who knows so much about football
and even more about being a grandfather.
F. P.

To Diego and Irene,
who rearrange my world.
R. C.

MADANI'S BEST GAME

Fran Pintadera • Raquel Catalina

translated by Lawrence Schimel

EERDMANS BOOKS FOR YOUNG READERS

GRAND RAPIDS, MICHIGAN

Our whole neighborhood knows it:
no one plays soccer like Madani does.
Even if there are two hundred kids out on the field,
he's easy to spot: he's the only one who plays barefoot.
Before him, the best player was whoever kicked the ball
the hardest. But then came Madani, and with him,
the best soccer we've ever seen.

Every Saturday, when the ball lands between his bare feet,
every passerby freezes. And not just them—the whole world does!
Waiters remain motionless with their trays held above their heads.
Old friends stop arguing. The pigeons don't fly.
Even traffic comes to a standstill!

10

This moment is when the show begins.

Madani makes the ball twirl
and passes it from one side to the other.

He hides it between his legs,

shrugs it over his shoulders,

catches it on his head,

then slides it down his back,

and drops it once more
between his bare feet.

Gooooal!

Everyone breaks into cheers!
The waiters toss their trays into the air,
the old friends jump up and hug one another,
and the pigeons take to the air in scattered flocks.

The shouts leave the playing field behind
and fill the whole neighborhood.

The sound crosses through doorways,
rushes past the magazine stand,
slips down alleyways,
swirls around the fountain,
and, growing fainter and fainter,
climbs the steps
up to Madani's house.

Barely a whisper remains now of that first celebration.
But Madani's mother hears it and feels proud.
She knows her son has scored a goal.
She would have liked to see it, but she still
has so many hems to let out and so many repairs left to make.
With a smile now, she keeps sewing.

When the game is over, everyone's exhausted—except for Madani.
He could play all week without stopping!
And without shoes!
Sometimes we like to imagine what Madani could do
if he only had a pair of good cleats.
Surely he would be even faster
and he might even be able to kick harder.
He might even manage that bicycle kick he tries every match.
He might even snatch the high balls away from Farola,
who's not only as tall as a lamppost, but also
the best player in the league—and on top of that,
the captain of our historic rival: the Southside team.

For a while now, Madani has been saving money in a metal tin.
Sometimes he skips buying an afternoon snack.
Other times, when we play an away game
and everyone else rides the bus, he walks instead.
And his tin box gets a little heavier with the money he saves.
"When it's full, I'll go shopping downtown!
And then our games will be better than ever!" he says each week.
The rest of us are happy; soon Madani will play
with a brand-new pair of cleats at last.

Tomorrow, our team will face Southside.
Even though it's a home game, we need to be ready.
Today was our last practice before the big match, but—
to everyone's surprise—Madani didn't even step onto the field.

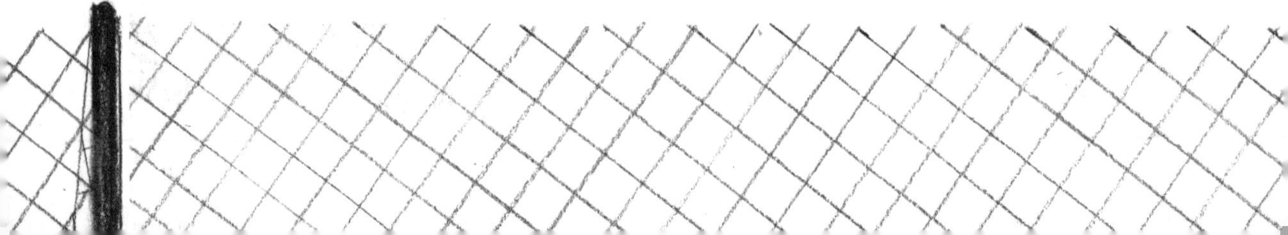

From the opposite sidewalk he shouted,
“I can’t practice today, guys. I’m going downtown!”
There was a moment of silence on the field as everyone
watched Madani walk away with the metal tin in his hand.

Practice was a disaster.
The forwards kicked air instead of the ball,
the midfielders couldn't land two straight passes,
and the goalie kept letting balls slip right through his legs.
And if that weren't enough—in our pickup game
against the retirees, we lost 1 to 7.

Still, our team didn't have any long faces.
All of us were thinking the same thing:
"Tomorrow . . . oh, tomorrow! Madani will give Southside
a real welcome with his new cleats!"

One hour before the big game, the whole team gathers.
We wait for Madani, to welcome him as a hero.
There he comes. He looks radiant.
He's wearing his green T-shirt with the number 14 on the back,
his black shorts,
and on his feet . . .

. . . on his feet are a pair of brand-new soccer cleats that are . . .

Invisible?!

“Madani, where are your shoes?” our team captain asks.
“What shoes? I always play this way,” Madani answers.
“Yeah, but . . . your shopping trip downtown? And the box?”
“Who said that was for cleats? I bought my mom a present! Now she’ll be able to finish her work faster and come watch me play every Saturday.

“Anyway, what are we waiting for? Are we going to play ball or what?”

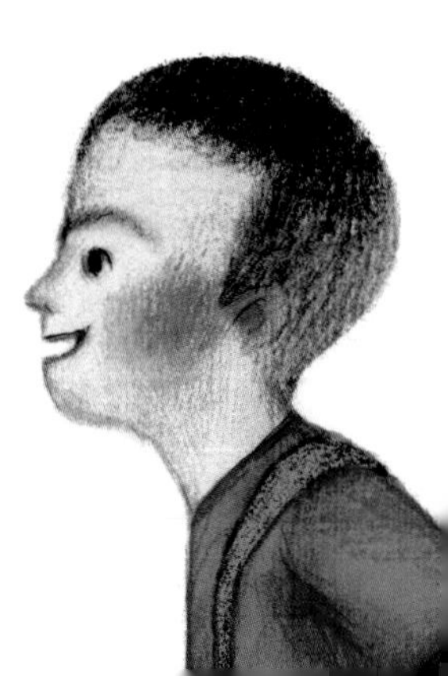

Migor SEWING MACHINES
SALE
OPEN

As we enter the field, to the excited shouts of the spectators,
everyone but Madani is still a bit confused.
But we suddenly wake up when we see the ball
speeding toward our goal.
One of our team, quick as lightning, crosses the field
to steal the ball. His T-shirt bears the number 14.
With the ball in his possession,
he dodges one, two . . . three opponents!
He takes position, raises his foot, and makes a flawless kick.

The park bursts into cheers. Madani is also proud of his goal.
He looks up at the stands, and there is his mother!
He raises his arms and runs toward her, as if this were the first goal he's ever made in his life.
"This goal is for you, Mom!"
"Thank you, my son! For the goal, for the sewing machine . . . and for everything else! Now, go play. There's still plenty of game left."

14

Before halftime, Madani's mother has applauded
her son's second goal. A real left kick!
He's scored a goal with each of his bare feet.

14

The match ends in a tie.
Farola scored goals by heading the ball
both times the Southside team had corner kicks.
Madani couldn't do anything against those high balls.
Nor could he run faster, or hit with more force than before.
And when he tried a bicycle kick, he made a fool of himself.
But no one cared.

Because now more than ever, everyone in the neighborhood knows . . .

There's no player like Madani!

NOTES FROM THE CREATORS

Before telling stories, I did many other things. For some years, I worked as a social educator in new immigrant housing. There I met a young boy named Madani and others like him.

Spending the afternoons playing with those kids made me remember the importance of the neighborhood and the stories that thrum in its streets.

Many years before, I was the one who played soccer in my neighborhood's central square.

Even though I put effort into it, I was never notable for my skill with the ball; instead, my abilities lay in writing poems and stories.

Things are the same today: I'm clumsy with a ball and wait on the sidelines with a pen and notebook.

As in this story about Madani, I like to write about the realities that are close at hand, which some call "the little things."

—F. P.

"Draw an angry face, a happy one, a sad one," an art book for children said, offering white outlines for readers to add the faces' emotions.

One day, all the wallpaper flowers in my parents' house had angry faces, happy faces, and sad faces . . . drawn at the height of a five-year-old girl.

I like to think my drawing on the wallpaper was not just a childhood prank, but foreshadowing. Years later, I studied fine art in Madrid and did a postgraduate degree in illustration in Valencia.

My path was not a straight line—there were side paths, jobs that had nothing to do with art, until I came back to books and drawing.

One day a manuscript reached my studio desk: "Our whole neighborhood knows it: no one plays soccer like Madani does." I thought back to my flowers, I saw the white space, I drew some bare feet, and the game began . . .

—R. C.

FRAN PINTADERA is a storyteller, theater director, and the author of over a dozen children's books. *Why Do We Cry?* (Kids Can) received a Parents' Choice Gold Award and was selected as a Bank Street College Best Book of the Year. *Madani's Best Game* was shaped by Fran's work in new immigrant housing, where soccer became a shared language for children from Senegal, Morocco, Mali, Algeria, and across the world. Fran lives in Spain. Follow him on Instagram @franpintadera.

RAQUEL CATALINA is a Spanish artist and illustrator whose books include *Benji's Blanket* (Green Bean). Her work has been exhibited in Spain, Mexico, Portugal, and Italy. In 2021, the original version of *Madani's Best Game* was selected as a NYPL Best Spanish-Language Book for Kids. Follow Raquel on Instagram at @raquelcatalinaillustration.

LAWRENCE SCHIMEL is the author of over 120 books and translator of over 130 books, including *Early One Morning* (Orca), *Niños*, and *One Million Oysters on Top of the Mountain* (both Eerdmans). His works have received many awards, including a PEN Translates Award and the GLLI Translated YA Book Prize Honor. Lawrence lives in Madrid, Spain. Follow him on Twitter @lawrenceschimel.

First published in the United States in 2022
by Eerdmans Books for Young Readers,
an imprint of Wm. B. Eerdmans Publishing Co.
Grand Rapids, Michigan

www.eerdmans.com/youngreaders

Text © 2021 Fran Pintadera
Illustrations © 2021 Raquel Catalina

Originally published in Spain as *La mejor jugada de Madani*
© 2021 Ediciones Ekaré, Barcelona, Spain

English-language translation © Lawrence Schimel 2022

All rights reserved

Manufactured in the United States of America

30 29 28 27 26 25 24 23 22   1 2 3 4 5 6 7 8 9

ISBN 978-0-8028-5597-8

A catalog record of this book is available from the Library of Congress

Illustrations created with with pencil, gouache, and colored pencil

Support for the illustration and translation of this book was provided by Acción Cultural Española, AC/E.
accioncultural.es